Marble Sky
Vuyelwa Carlin

seren

Seren
is the book imprint of
Poetry Wales Press Ltd
Nolton Street, Bridgend, Wales
www.seren-books.com

© Vuyelwa Carlin, 2002

The right of Vuyelwa Carlin
to be identified as the Author of this Work
has been asserted in accordance with the
Copyright, Designs and Patents Act, 1988.

ISBN 1-85411-300-3

A CIP record for this title is available from
the British Library

All rights reserved. No part of this publication
may be reproduced, stored in a retrieval system,
or transmitted at any time or by any means
electronic, mechanical, photocopying, recording
or otherwise without the prior permission
of the copyright holders.

The publisher works with the financial assistance of the
Arts Council of Wales

Cover Image: Detail of a painting by Elfyn Lewis

Printed in Palatino by
Creative Print and Design Wales, Ebbw Vale

LLYFRGELLOEDD SIR DDINBYCH DENBIGHSHIRE LIBRARIES	
C4600000342761	
L B C	14/06/2004
AFIC 821.914	£6.95
	RL

Contents

Bottles of Blood

Bottles of Blood	9
The Memorial Service	10
My Mother's House, Johannesburg	12
Shellhead	13
A Filter of Nerve	14
Gold Watch	16
Frangipani, Uganda	17
And Then	18
Cold Places	19
Tail-wind over the Atlantic	20
Cloudscape over Seattle	21
Warsaw Beggars	22
Look On My Works	23
Polish Wedding	24
Jezyk Polski	25
Lake Czos, Poland	26

The Marble Sky

Identical	29
Holy Fruit	30
Vase of Grasses for a Truthteller	34
Fear of Wind	35
The Marble Sky	36

January Nightingales

Mary Magdalene in the Easter Garden	41
The Physicist's Easter Vigil	42
Good Friday Swans on the Water Meadow	43
Music	44
Birdsong	45
January Nightingales	46
The Green Boy	47
August Bales in Moonlight	49
By Mad Dog Farm	50
By Mad Dog Farm (2)	51
Escape of Two Pigs	52
The Man in the Straw Hat	53
The Flying Lesson	54
The Anchorite	57
Acknowledgements	63

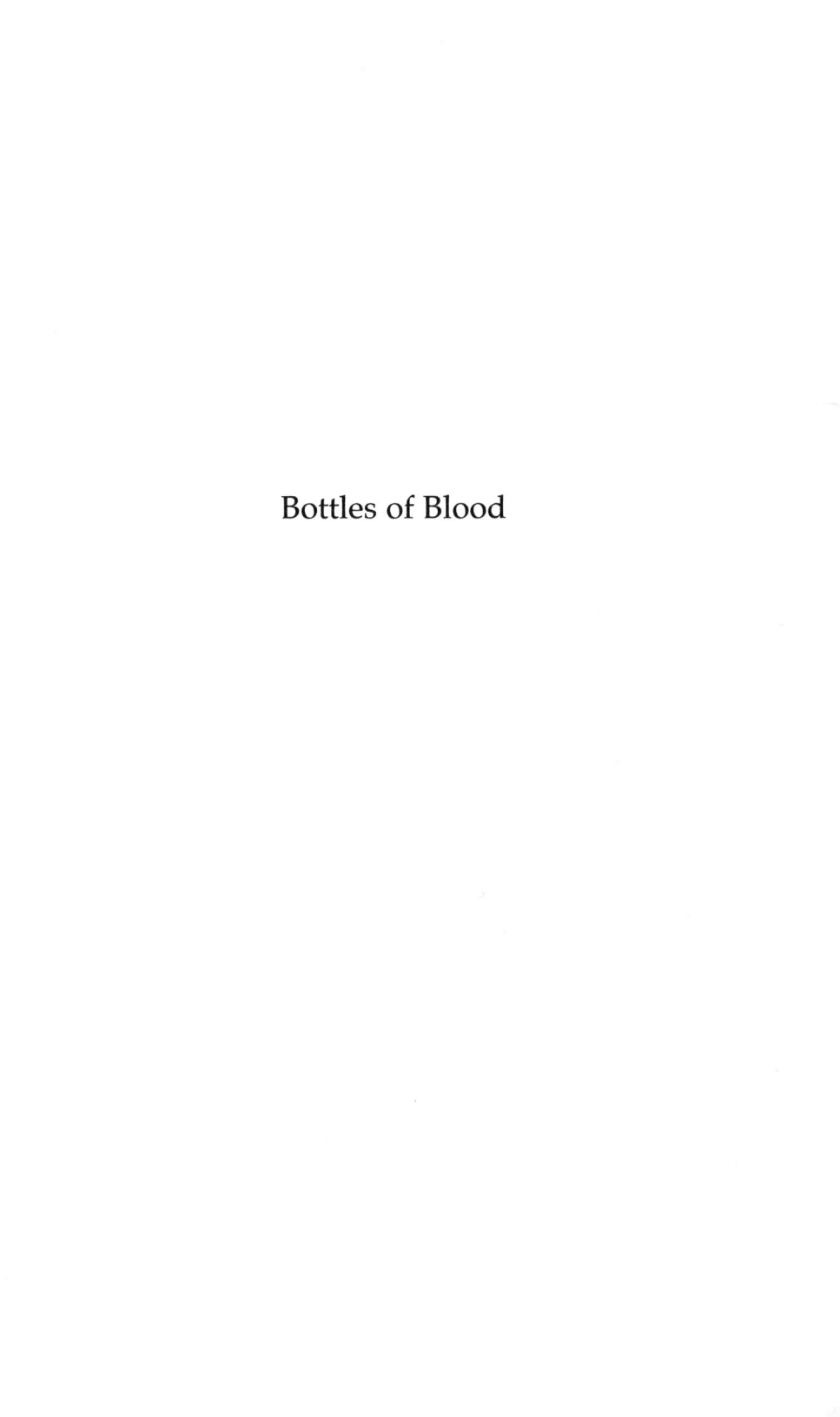

Bottles of Blood

Bottles of Blood
Uganda, c. 1958

Forty years ago
you had a job, blood-collecting.
You, and an orderly, drove through the dust,
the vivid dusty green, some of it near-jungle,
to young mens' colleges, crates
of bottles rattling in the back.

The boys lay on pallets,
grimacing for show, while the hearty,
thick, quick blood slid into the bottles:
then up, and back to work –
no rest, or tea. They crowded
to give; the children, in clusters,

bobbed at the windows,
enjoying the afternoon's bleeding.
On the way home the low sun glared;
the bottles' clatter was more subdued now –
more a clunk. The blood swayed,
pools of velvet, stirring purple.

The Memorial Service

1. Kampala and Port Bell, Uganda

The old Hindu crematorium, high-walled and grassy:
the open pyre, butter placed in your mouth –

no! we stayed away. Next morning – bright
as Eden, still cool – we scooped ash

into a paper bag; dropped dewy flowers
on all the earths, particles, powders.

Then to Port Bell: home of Bell beer, dark
in its black bottles – sits like stone, you said,

quaffing of an evening on the front steps.
Your ashes were cast on the lake.

And they have swirled in those waterways:
twirled with corpses in the terrible times.

2. St Mary's Church, Shropshire

Thirty years ago I watched you depart,
across the neighbours' back garden, rapidly,

swinging your arms, intent.
The shadow of me knew this was it –

the fascinating journey, at last:
– No God – but the beauty of Death! – you'd said.

We told our tales of you, in this ancient space,
its elegance of light, and arch.

You were elusive, mostly, as ever:
but your dry, pitiless vanishing was held

in these stones, sunk in green:
this place of precious oils poured upon the head.

My Mother's House, Johannesburg

22 Hoylake Road, Greenside: I tread the vague house,
pick out its layout; and the garden

with the great swathe of roses down the front,
the fig trees, and the black metal cat faces.

A house strung with your intense, wounded girlhood:
fat scrapbooks of loves – film stars, royal family;

diaries of desperate loves – teachers, mostly.
Who loved you? You used to tell of a dream:

you were in the empty house, playing –
the empty rosy garden, playing –

gradually unease, that dream-malaise,
crept in from the edges,

the only reality, terrible paw swiping at repose:
then you were on your bed, and it came to you

that your mother lay dead, under it.
That fey, deaf woman, shut away in dreams

– except the stubby earth-hands, nails full of earth –
how fragile she was! how fragile you all were:

triad of tomb-flowers, crumbled at a touch –
when you died they were dust; not dead, but dust.

I remember the smell of old writings, old dolls –
Violet the precious, her ancient silks, her porcelain head.

Shellhead

1. Your father grew to love you, in the end –
   had wanted a son, though.

   So you wanted girls, and more girls:
   when the cute boy was born, "I shrieked in horror!"

   Luckily, he was a charmer –
   blue eyes, dimples, endless smiles

   – and weeping – he was always soft, bruisable;
   roared with anguish at the beggars' fungused feet,
   at Oliver, beaten for gruel.

2. You told this dream, once –
   a crooked house, labyrinthine –

   and you came upon him, cherub in a bathtub,
   his head all mollusced,
   a cap of limpets; you touched one and it opened –

   inside, a grey comma, thread of woken worm.
   – Poor baby, boy, man!

   struggling in your dream-pool,
   its grotesque fish, the icy truth of it.

A Filter of Nerve

You sit in the past, indestructible –
every thought, half-thought,
the little underthoughts that twinkle away down tributaries

– scarce-flash of silver –
all known – by time, by electrons, by God –
all set, for ever.

Known, but not knowable:
memory visits; sees through a filter of nerve,
over gulfs of synapses. – We dream strangely

of the past, the dead:
reality outside reason, or language.
Words try, in dreams – sometimes – a mould, attempted,

of water, an endless fiddling with air –
but no mix: the dream-reality old,
old as time, or beyond;

the word-reality – reason's blocks –
still an imposition: the other slips between
– blizzard-snow blowing through shanty walls.

So, you: real – for always – a carving
through thirty-nine years, accurate to the last dream –
but gone: quite inaccessible.

You surface, changed – drifted over
with brain-dust.
It has a sort of truth, this web, this feathering:

deep to deep: the odd fish
in the abyss six miles down know each other.
The chill of you

calls to the chill of me: a figure in a bus,
stepping down unwillingly;
a house, night pressing against the curtainless windows.

Gold Watch

A good gold – 24 carat? –
as yellow-gleaming as thirty years ago
– Vadgama's, Kampala; my raptures:

I was reminded, in Tiffany's –
one piece per velvet cushion; compositions –
real bulbs, a Delft boy, a tiny diamond dragonfly.

The rationalist told Jung
of her dream of a gold scarab;
as she spoke, it banged against the pane,

the brilliant thing: and she was freed
from the chance chaining,
the blind sprawl, splashing onto land:

could ponder, at least, fooleries: –
the singularity of jokes;
the forgiveness-prayer, found on the Belsen baby.

Plump sphere, soft gold,
rich-looking on night-blue –
a posthumous present, paid for over months:

half-sense of soul-streams –
the universe is nothing now – wherever you like,
faster than electrons, you just go.

I lost the watch, once:
for weeks it glinted in the grass,
little heavy ball,

gold pip, dewy, with its stilled microscopic gems.
The country jeweller admires it –
healing gold, gold roller – "a lovely piece".

Frangipani, Uganda

The spongy wood of them – hardly like wood –
texture of rottenness; that papery bark;

the white, gold flowers, their sticky milk:
flower-pictures on the grass, mine a frangipani angel.

I had a sense of them, suddenly,
from those years ago – recall the scent, scentlessly;

the stored shape of it, the held ghost:
as the soul remembers the flesh, perhaps –

walking spaceless in the gone gullies of mind:
an echo of leaf, an equation of breeze.

And Then

The other dead, the rest of the dead,
who went as they ought – old, resigned, surprised, –

they have touched delicately already
from time to time, as best they can –

an indication on the breeze, some grey evening,
anticipating time's end, or sooner:

grace; clarity; charm of each held structure.

When it comes to you it is different.
I feel like Echo, pining invisible

after the harsh beautiful flower:
antiquity's stony cruelty! gods no better than us,

unredeemed: we meet on tundra, deep iron.

Cold Places

1. The wounded East, its deep winters –
   the bleak, blown places:

   you loved the African heat,
   loved it vitally, like a lizard,
   basking to live –

   wanting to be warmed through
   to the old, frozen earths.

2. At Mikolajki the swans land,
   slide on the river-runway with a fast tailwind –

   how icy it is! –
   far-journeyed, freighted still with the dead.

3. From these stones
   a whirling concentration, a startling spin,
   leaps out – almost chemical –

   of pain, and fear:
   these blocks are soaked with it.

4. An old, old child's wish –
   lake after lake, mile-deep –
   four feet of ice, and the winter rails laid:

   on forest edges, in forest-clearings,
   snow lies on frigid dust;

   commemoration stones – or none –
   a pattern of dots; a map of the dead.

Tail-wind over the Atlantic

Wind almighty, six miles up –
we watched films, grimly:
roar of engines, roar of wind, all night long!

We surfed breakers of wind,
bounced on wind-billows: (and that far black sea,
almost shipless –

how empty still, our azure lump of star):
I almost enjoyed the ride,
forgot – for specks of time – the black waters.

We blew in early:
in the dawn (the wind blowing hard, but steadier)
I looked down: Ireland,

terrier-shape on the curved sea –
as it looked when the fur-clothed, sinless few
straggled dark against the snow:

the laws of faithful matter, veiled;
a silence of equation;
the winter palaces, vast, untrodden, of those hunters.

Cloudscape over Seattle

Into cloud, a cloudscape –
cloud piled on cloud, solid, pearl-white, white-white;
cloud throwing shadow on cloud:

and we passed under the legs of cloud-Colossi,
by towers of cloud-castles, cloud cathedral-arches;
Cloud City, built of cloudstone:

good old springy fluff,
like cotton bolls – child-cloud, where we bounced
– as we slid down the blue ice of glaciers, on blankets:

below, the lush, leafy city – peopled speck
in the blue, and green: and the dark, dark empty seas,
white-trailed with ship – with the odd, rare ship.

Warsaw Beggars

It is all avoidance – they creep, weep,
hug knees: are alien as reptiles,

their eyes, reptile eyes. They hate us –
we are fleshly cash machines,

the working of us a complex, tiring business:
the constant push, squeeze, of emotion –

not for fun, but because the men are waiting.
The walking children have learned –

their eyes skew off, like the adults'.
If we caught a chin, stared into the dark eyes? –

impossible! They kiss, stroke,
yet they are utterly curled away:

even the babies – each one carries a baby,
a stiff bundle, turned away, held away.

Look On My Works
Hitler's bunker, Ketrzyn, Poland

Snowy paths,
and the birch trees – such beauty,
whispering over closed souls,

souls like stones,
presenting no doors: those smiles,
those absences, terrible:

twice-bombed, in the end –
the blocks buckled,
cracked – steel fingers sprang out.

*

Smell of black drip, silence –
compare, remember
Warsaw, the Old Town,

its precise reconstructing,
to the last faded-pink frontage:
the metal segment

built into the saint's south wall,
where the tanks smashed in,
hurtled through iconed lofts.

Polish Wedding

Food kept coming, all night:
first a gleaming soup, full of *makaron* –
a padding of wall for the whirling mad vodka.

We danced in lines and rings, whooped –
then a polonaise – pair after pair,
dipping and arching, oranges and lemons,

following-my-leader; the master
weaving a gracious weave, disposing – pat-a-pit pat –
the clumsy English here, there; up; down.

After Jane Austen, the belly-and knee-games,
blindfold: the Pram Dance –
money thrown in bowls, a jig with a newly-wed.

The Dairy Hall was all streamered –
that day's bright twists; and paler ones
coming out of curl – remnants, dusts.

The old trains rattle past,
by grove-spoils, half-secret –
the not-so-deep dead, pressing, pressing
                    into the feast-bread.

Jezyk Polski
The Polish Language

Consonant-clusters: swish of snow,
of wind, laden with snow-powder; and ice –

the creak of it, deep, as the deeps knit,
grind and crunch in the lake-space grown too small:

a dense tongue, then: narrow runnels of vowels,
threads of boreholes,
bound in with snow-muscle, rustle of crystals:

it is lips stretched sideways,
a song of teeth, snug cheeks – guarding, surely,

the little sacs, the warm, tiny fractals'
microscopic dancing bloods,
from their clay's bleak tilt.

Lake Czos, Poland

The top water, the meltwater,
unclamps, clamps; the weeds sleep, half the year,
and fish hang, half-animate,

blood an ice-slush. The fishers are lumps of patience,
or of cold: each has chipped, hewn,
hauled out a blue plug – translucent, basso;

sits out the winter
over groan, and yaup. But now is summer,
and we swim in mild, wild water

fringed with birch, birchy mounds –
this is low-hill country:
the soft weeds are rooted in ever-cold.

The dead rustle; in winter
the wind whips them about, they drift in the drifts –
legion, brushing the dark; desolation-smoke.

The Marble Sky

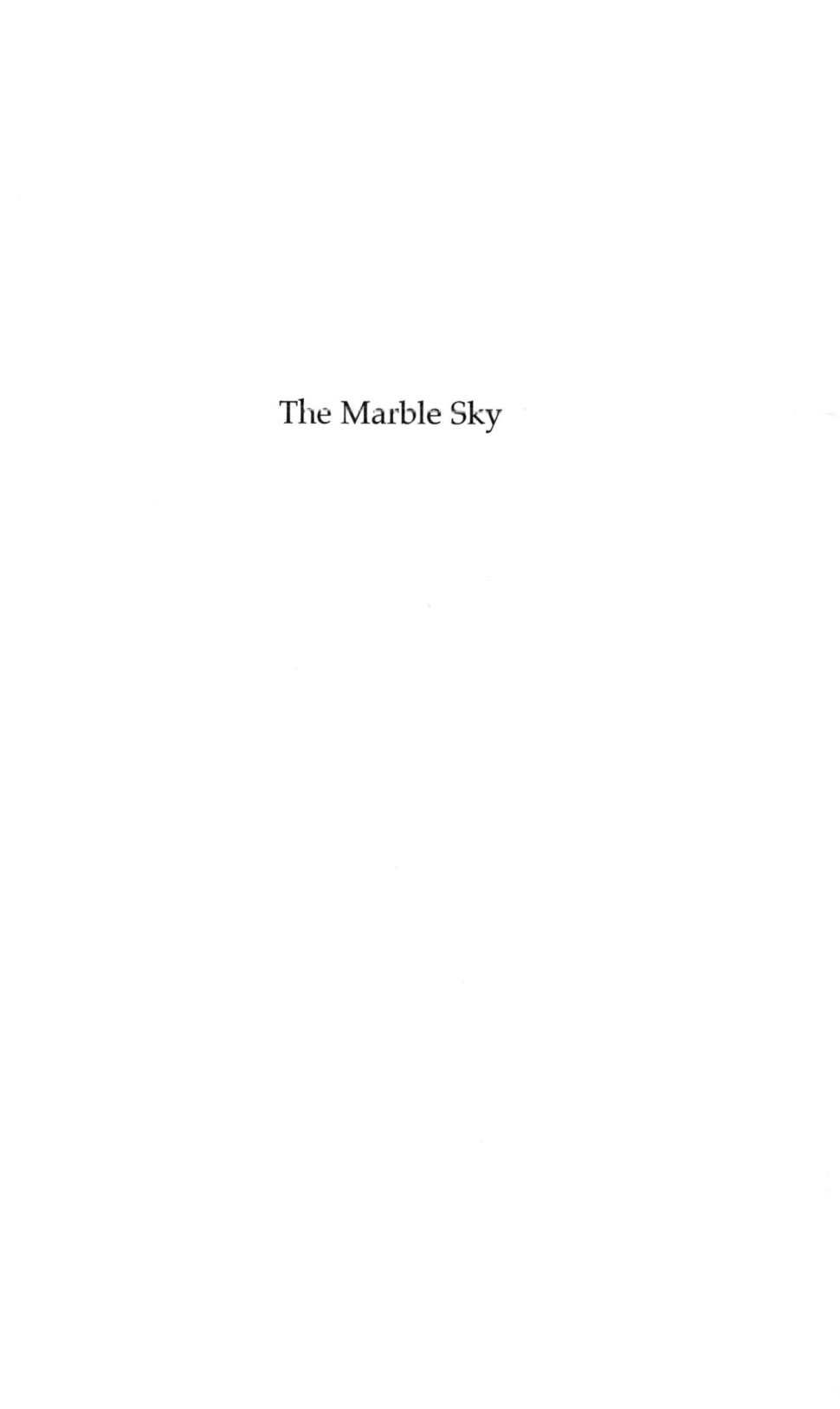

Identical

1. He's thinner in the face, a little,
   and the hair – you can tell;
   the other is tougher, wins cups.

   Disinter their old bones,
   no test could tell. They could collude –
   who fathered whom?

   Their sparking nerves
   have a sympathy – the split mass
   pulling together.

   The fitful grounds of stuff
   never forget – once interacting,

   light-years sped apart,
   are altered for eternity
   (eternity? that steel ball, Earth-size,

   worn away by a fly's foot
   landing each million years: – the start of it).

2. Doubles, singletons:
   the tenderer, the boss man;

   play of feature, the same –
   and could you tell whose grey-blue eyes?

   But each ghost twines
   through its mesh – curvets,
   unmistakable – the ripple of him, and him,

   – no matter, the interchangeable bones –
   patterns of soul; each dust's subtle whorl.

Holy Fruit

James and Edward, identical twins: James was severely damaged during birth; Edward cared for him for many years, until, in their middle age, James died.

1. Hill-walks

I can walk the fields again, the hills –
climb up to the piny silences,
as I did forty years ago, treading over the dead.

Do I miss you, James? We were one once –
a singleton, pre-soul: and when I am dead,
no test, none, will tell.

We were the two mad men –
one simple, one a scholar:

and yes, I am full of knowledge, an historian,
and dreamer – but is that so wonderful?

How gold the larch, how delicate the gold birch:
where are the still waters? did we find them, ever?

2. Stylite

A gravity, a soul-touch –
it was you I sensed, in the blowy garden;
fingers of wind in a harp – a fleeting thin music,

but no plucking. Such grace
from the despised, the suffered –

yes, you were suffered: bluefish,
born stiff as a board, pressed to Death's heart.

The stylite rots on his pillar year on year,
bitten with hemp: a mad, harsh saint! –
his God a garden of stone.

We dreamers are dealers in stones,
love the closed lustres.

3. Silverpoint

Chaste, spare, the picture within the picture:

you were poor and simple – as a church mouse,
as the first Franciscans, jesters of God,
in the ruined Portiuncola.

At your grave, these windy days,
arranging my bouquets of berries;

while you breathed I lacked generosity,
presented polished facets.

4. Into the labyrinth

But now the bloodthread drags,
tugs on raw roots.

Into the dark of the other
I should have ventured long ago – we two, beggars
on your unknown road.

Well, the year pulls on –
hoarfrost, white thick mists. But I thaw,
with pain: so it must be.

You had no theories! had the run of the garden.
The labyrinth, the whirlwind,
the green field – our lodging is all of them.

I could have eaten holy fruit: eaten with you,
the dark, the bitter, the delicious.

Vase of Grasses for a Truthteller

These grasses remind me of you –
young man, forever truthteller:
your world is stones – or gems –
a garden of statuary – exquisite, coarse,

blind, it's all one.
You scrutinised grass – it was handy,
perfection of plane: later, you lay
– lost, we thought – among the beanpoles:

straights, simplicities.
"One entire and perfect chrysolite" –*
if only! – or granite, or thrown clays'
earthen lot, unmoving –

your perfect world. What is Echo,
twanging the soul? charge of thought, thought-rush,
walking on water? the wrenched, ringing word
sailing on the edge of the wind?

Truthteller, truthteller –
metaphor a lie among your stones; – but cruel,
this garden – changeable
as sands, gases; the laws,

the pure laws, stream elsewhere. You yearn after them,
unquestioning, in a world without wonder:
– but who says so? only a little younger,
you ran, flapping arms,

open to take-off as a newborn.
The electricities veer and jib, unkind –
but all our lost paths still wend, for you –
everyday as grass; incorruptible.

> * the quotation is from *Othello*

Fear of Wind

*"Did you not hear the storm? The wind tore at the wall,
the great tower gate yawned like a lion
on its creaking hinges."*
                    Wislawa Szymborska 'Tower of Babel'

What is this fear of wind? –
it roars, to be sure – how the trees,
the turbulent night sea of them,

sway and swish, the little branches whirling –
here will be rugs of yew,
carpets of applewood, pearwood.

Intense quiets; black wells of quiet;
then the approaching charge,
the tidal wave, the war-cry,

beating on your powerless dark:
the world rocks, and tilts –
you fear like mad: as sailors did, once,

the great pouring over the edge,
the rush into the void
of the little, little twigs of ships.

The Marble Sky

"Yond marble heaven" – Othello

> *"You lack the sense of taking part.*
> *No other sense can make up for your missing*
> *sense of taking part."*
>   Szymborska, 'Conversation with a Stone'

1. A changeling, strangeling –
   old tales, I pleased myself –
   beautiful Kay, the ice-chip in his heart,

   sitting in the palace blue with ice,
   placing the ice polygons this way, that.

2. Exquisite achromatism of eye
   – water grey perhaps,
   or the limpid arm-depth of lake-ice below the white:

   at six months – common age of no fear –
   I couldn't catch it; you turned away,

   and turned away –
   a shadow in the grove, fleeting, and Panic.

3. The world in a blade of grass!
   – an hour's study,
   and this before you could walk:

   a long barn roof, clean against the sky;
   crows landing, raucous rags

   spoiling the line; you cry, caw,
   a little cawing fury, far down:
   what do they care, in their high thinbone clarities?

4. The Pythagorous-game: –
   a stick placed upright in soil, another leaned against it,
   delicately balanced hypotenuse:

   to you, it was no game –
   to you, it was life; lifeblood, the Law.

5. The marble sky,
   frozen sea, stone fish, of the past:
   you knew where you were, there –

   but had to press on
   in bafflement of blood; the nerve paths,
   that for you were skittish,

   their patterns alien; you were alien,
   even to yourself – bloodbead, nerve-bead, strung
   askew.

6. The ancient, green roads
   slipping from perception;

   rocks torn from the sun
   that the sun still recognises – old star,
   old whorls of star-gas:

   the same stuff yet different –
   what ruffled your energies,
   turning (it seemed) the wolf-pelt inwards?

7. Pinewoods wrap you in dusk,
   dead-branchiness; deeps of unquizzy browncurl:

   Kaspar Hauser, stranger, riddler;

the Wild Boy of Aveyron – his peace
was to sip a glass of water, watch the moon:

puzzles of sharps,
scatters of ice-shards, and who knows the lie of them?

8. Opaqueness; blockworld;
   I glimpse your landscape, bump against its
                                     word-casts –

   in your nineteenth year, Father Christmas
   still teetered on frosty tiles, scrabbled in chimneys.

   The curve of Time; the odd loopback
   – fizz of future-present:
   is that why densities charmed, weighting the palm?

9. The tiny, the slowest – they tangle, old hands,
   with the graces of things, atomless.

   Were you avalanched-upon, stunned?
   the airy sanctuaries infilled?
   – the cattle-cars trundling eternally, that dead-cold?

10. Who reads you, though, cold? who dares?
    the grey gelid weight
    presses into spaciousness, crushes the pure thin walls –

    the suffering servant, like it or not.
    You have strange laws –
    beaten out as best you could;

    as you knocked up against a solid sky,
    fingered carvings of concepts; Etruscan glyphs,
                                            uncodes.

January Nightingales

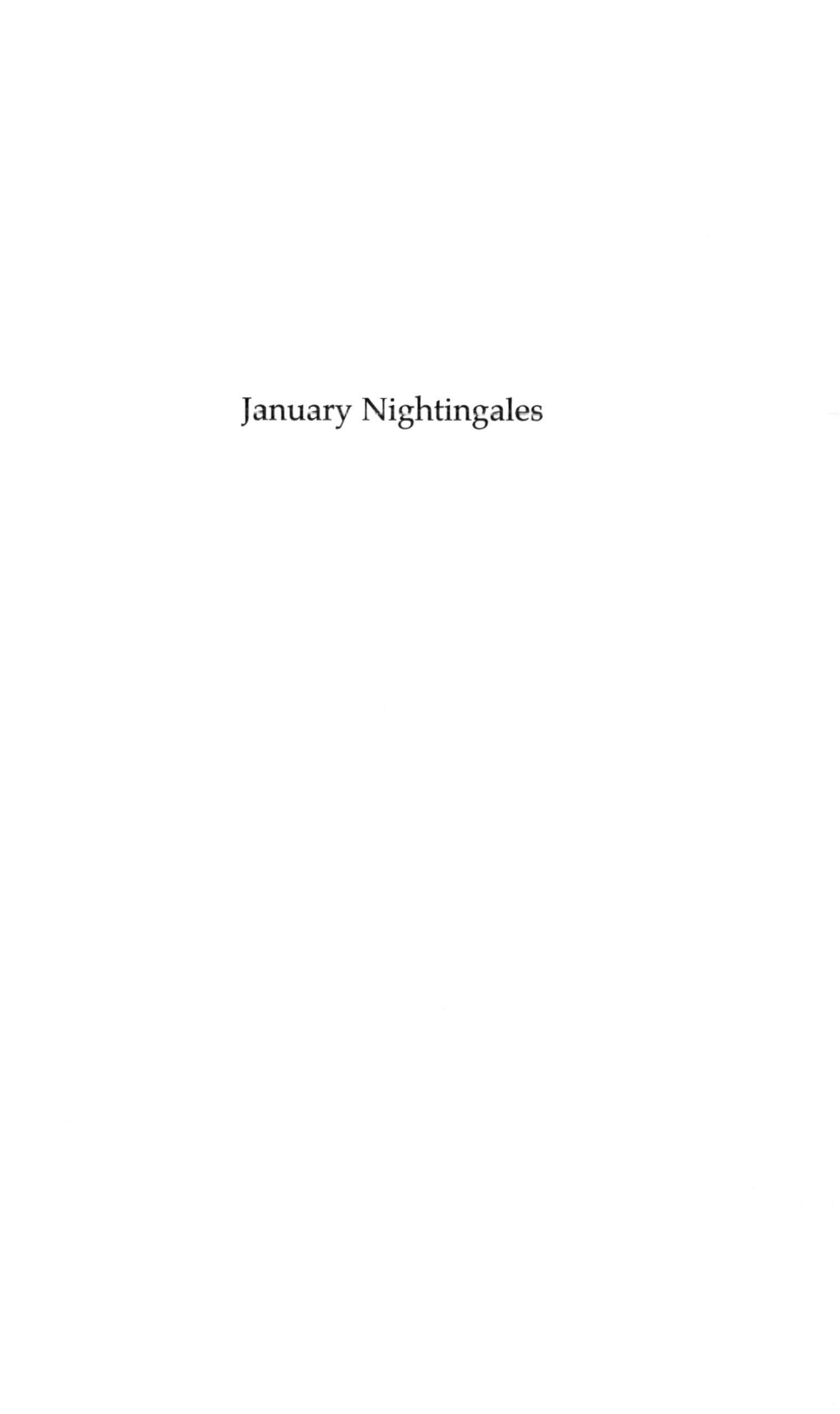

Mary Magdalene in the Easter Garden

What did she do, those hours of racketing dark?
Did she wander like a madwoman,
declaiming in the streets, among the flying tiles?

The morning perhaps was bright – blown, brilliant –
a world of bright pieces, thrown together anyhow:

wind swishing in the trees like the waters of chaos –
wind in the empty tomb, the whistle of it.

Push on through whirligig shrubs, try to see it –
the clay of God, rethrown –
clothes flapping, feet chilly in the wet –

how could it hook up with the mind's eye,
this tangle of old dusts? Through the slow hours,

the quiver again of atoms; eyes, prickled with light;
threads of thought: "Before Abraham –
before Abraham was, I am": that was certain, now:

and she, among tumbled garden tools,
seeing, and not seeing: wind-scourged newness,
toughening, amazed, in the fresh air.

The Physicist's Easter Vigil
For John Polkinghorne

"Mathematics is the language of the universe,
the speech of God. Yes, we can speak to God,
read what he writes in his own hand.
What is matter's nature, in words? – it is absurdity.

"A theorem of the resurrection? that mighty revamp
in the stone, in the silence of God,
of the cold, heavy clay,
of our loved dying flesh? This was no jump-start,

"but a turning away from the attractor death,
energies moving into a new coherence –
dispersible, streaming through the vast spaces –
doors, walls, universes.

"Holy Saturday, this long vigil:
I ponder the particles that are God,
the searing of God into this history, this garden –
the man in the garden, ungrasped at first by tired earth."

Good Friday Swans on the Water Meadow

The pain of the world – and of other soul-studiers,
who knows? – and now evening:
the river is still, but the field-lake rocks –

the swans are playing. They flap, honk,
walk water – break free of water-tension,
the drag of skin – fly low, madly,

zoom down on a long ski. Our world of signs, charms: –
these feathercraft, such hauteur –
now this strange, redwater clowning: secret mesh,

its beating heart – we call it to us
with player words, uncontingent.
It will make no supplication –

it is no-self, its heart is stone.
– Your eyes, jet beads, tar-balls;
but you have no *you*, or *I*. Purpling water clings,

the airs toss, stretch: shoals of matter,
all one: again, the buffeting,
the great feet climbing the spray-stair, the air-ladder.

Music

And if there are no ears to hear?
no dancing tiny bones – little movers and shakers –
no nerve-grove where the music room is?

A music machine in the desert –
miles and miles of emptiness: the waves travel on,
encountering no aural systems:

unshaped data; raw stuff;
gipsy waves: dispersing in disarray against rocks,
blown through by brisk sandy winds.

Music does not exist – say musicians –
until it is heard: notes hang on the page,
silent tools – not like words,

punching the heart. Yet music – like numbers –
was always there: we found it.
How else do you explain perfect pitch?

Music in the desert: rocks, sand, quiver –
with what stone-communion? and the caravans of waves –
what other encounters? what keener ears?

Birdsong

Cheep, wuckoo, chirrup: ur-pipings:
they pull, push, at our tongues, throats –

we strive for little crude sound-sculptures.
The perfection of cold chants: not heartless –

heartless is neither here nor there: they are other
as trees, green stalks – what music unheard

in those green, woody pipes?
They call and call – not for us. We love them:

it's nothing to them. The same phrase over and over,
we say – pressing them, little air-bones,

into shapes of Thought: but there's no holding them,
first harmonists; note-catchers.

Malleus, incus, stapes – latecomers,
last-minute developments, instruments of theory:

we chase music, make it conscious.
The first fliers, flapping leathers,

called harshly – if they called at all:
then the whittling down, hollowing out, warming up;

the feathering, the carving of horn: given back,
the whistles of wind, water, in stony, earthy channels.

January Nightingales

A richness extraordinary, of chirrup and trill
– late that night – two of them:

yawn, ears! like an old lion mad in his cage
yearning for what is beyond –

life flung profusely, great gobbets of it:
oodles, lashings, of quavers, chirps!

You have mistimed: these nights are cool, like April.
A thousand miles to the East,

the lakes are frozen; colourless ice feet-thick,
each fisherman stoic by his hole,

a dark swaddle: but – they say –
the winters are kinder now; not what they were.

Tiny wisps of foolery, twinges of tragedy,
twirl in the garden with your intense cold charms.

The Green Boy

Yes: the rumour
you heard is true; there was
a green boy here –
found – oh,

twelve years back –
moss-eyed
watcher by a sunk forest
path-thread; I

took him by a cool
emerald hand; – he seemed
not to mind; – took him
to be mine;

lessoned him; in the end
he could talk; – read, spell:
– but that first winter he
called a halt, was

slow, pale, chill; – I
agonied! – but with March,
April, he greened
again, learned; – so! I understood,

let him be, inly furled
from the cold; – other times
between my hands
he skilled, even smiled –

(burnished laurel-
dark lips) – never say
he was not happy
here! – Well,

he should stay outdoors I felt:
– he labours now
on a farm, some few miles
from me; – (his winter

fallowing,
kindly and somewhat
proud they all know of,
round here): – I often

go there, gate-leaned
watch him, gain,
conscientious; fern-
skinned.

– He is grave; but if I wave
enough, call, smile,
he will raise, from afar,
his green arm in the end.

August Bales in Moonlight

Once a year make a point of it –
the full-mooned field, the bales;
sit on a bale. The hungry mind, wanting snakejaws –

that old tale of torment, what is it? –
voracious hunger,
and a needle-throat. Beauty pours –

we catch snippets, crumbs.
These colours have no names! – cloud, whitish, lit;
bales, suggesting – or is it memory? – lion-gold.

Poor thoughts, cramped runners, dream-runners;
struggling in light,
racked with not-black shadows; wrestling.

By Mad Dog Farm

Creature of the dell, yellow-eyes;
helpless guardian, raving on your chain,
of the low road, the empty road,
the empty, dipping fields:

the rare, solitary walker,
the half-seen leap of hare,
the noiseless badger, slashing your sleep –
these are the monsters, the monstrous tormentors.

And the moon, when it glares,
a white-pouring ball;
then you are desperate – yell, hurtling,
clinking: far silvery cattle stir.

By Mad Dog Farm (2)

Starkbough; road filmed with ironwater:
the dog – my dog – drags,
pulls back; anguish swirls in his nostrils,
old pains not yet rotted down:

he sees the bare barn wall, capers.
– Staring-eyes, sinless
in your dungeon of sky, hills,
you are gone – dead, somewhere:

a spin of atoms, and who holds the pattern of you,
your poverty, madness, your dog-thoughts?
Is there comfort? – your roughlump of soul,
inchoate, heavy laden?

Escape of Two Pigs

A revolt; animal power;
they smelt the blood; were having none of it.

Trotter-tracks by the river, made under the moon
– they hid by day, it seemed –

the odd dawn sighting, probably imagined:
there was a mythic feel to it,

of copsy voices just missed,
horn-scored trees. May the long grass still hide them,

those mysterious lives; rudiments,
fragments, echoes, of souls.

The Man in the Straw Hat

In the little, summer train
– dreaming greens going by,
with vetch, willowherb, queen
of the meadow – I sit: who am I?

I am no farmer – look at my hands
(but my face could say otherwise –
it is a face of past, present,
future; it is rosy, and puzzles).

I was on the train years ago
when the old man leaned forward, grave,
and asked you "Can you tell me
if Isaac Griffiths is still alive?"

Am I, perhaps, the guardian
of the line – the good ghost?
Look at the wheat, on the turn
to gold; the dog-roses, massed!

The Flying Lesson

A child's book, "The Magic Chair";
we sat on the air, bouncing on it –
the strength, the springiness!
one understood, up there, it was stuff,

not nothing: not quite nothing –
"A little thing, the size of a hazel nut,
in the palm of my hand...
all that is made." Down below

– not far – the bluebells,
blue-purple pools, spreads, mantles,
lay – beauty elemental, thoughtbreaking –
on the hills, the sparse woods' floors.

Verse 2 quotes from Dame Julian of Norwich's
'Revelations of Divine Love'.

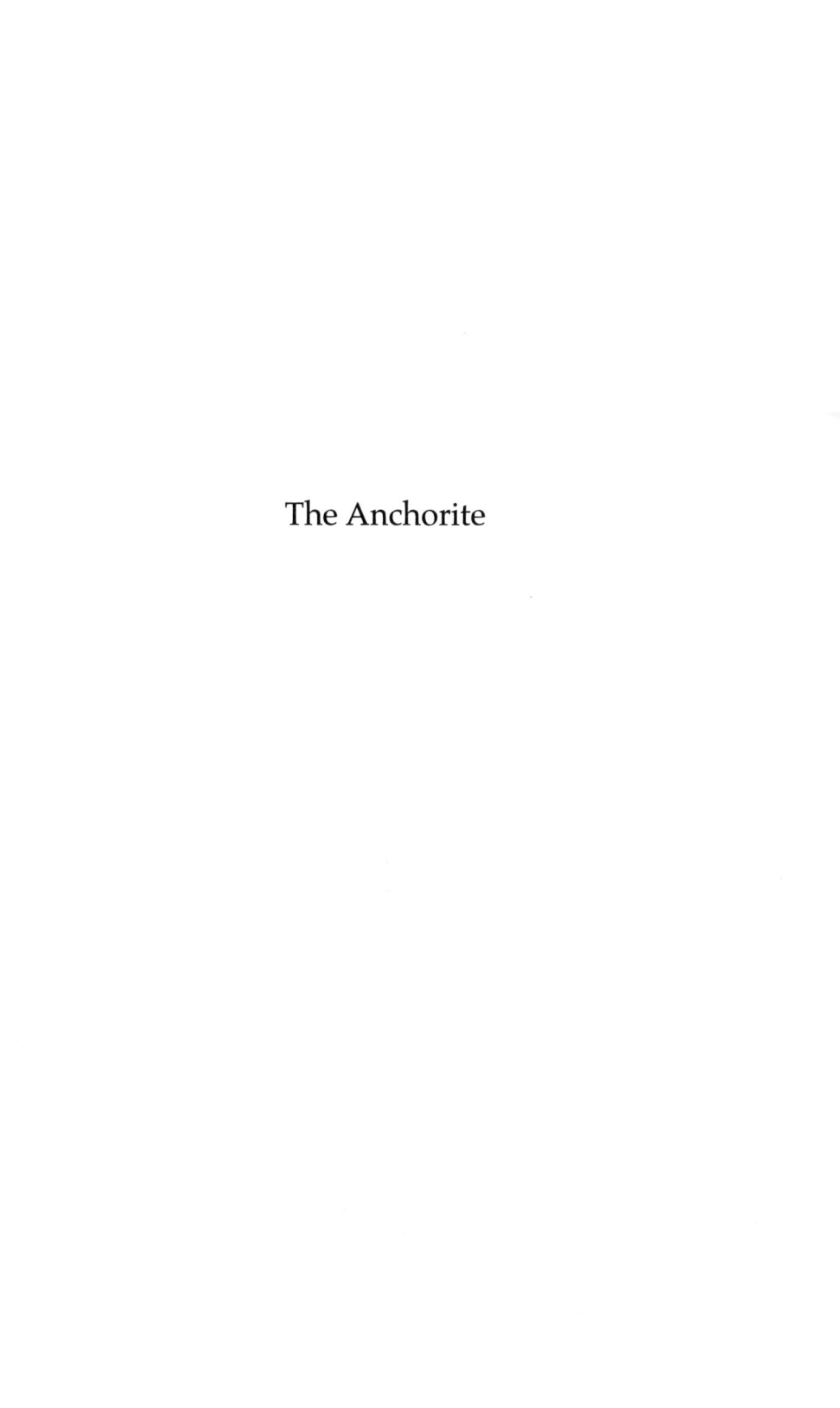

The Anchorite

The Anchorite

1. Elation

At last, here I am: my garden laid out;
this white interior flushed like a seashell,
beating with sunset; – my cell
sits by a hill, hummocky,
the sides roughly stepped. It is Iron Age,
a fort – little thorn trees on top
twisted with wind; black pools.

Already I have lain there,
watching the stars: thanking God,
fascinated by God,
who knows every electron intimately,
each mind to the ancient, common depths:
oh the wind of God, scouring everything!

2. Silence

This straw, its terrible frailty:
fantastical troops crowd – have always crowded,
the brave and strong! We talk,
as we have always talked, of shadows,
imaginary places,
where keen winds blow, polishing the soul –
the desert as I thought it would be,
exhilarating bareness, a stark beautiful rock.

It is falling away, all of it –
the romance, the dreams, the opinions:
no ecstasy, only a dull fear,
the great dull emptiness of the universe.

We are down to the bones: God, and I.
The silence of it is too much for me.

3. Accidie

I walk my poor garden, noting the weeds grow,
the shadow-patterns day after day.
My prayers cling about me, cannot shake free –
a stiff clay, pushed with stiff hands.
What old fierce rooted thing blocks my path?

Is this the soul's dark night?
I thought it would be exciting – knight-errantry,
a push through a mysterious land,
by lightless lakes and stern heathy hills.

I feel I could wrestle with God
– something grand: but this stifling,
this bone-idleness!

4. Poverty

The old mad beggar, remember him?
the green boy, his green arms, alone,
raising his arm to us, strangers?
They walk along the road of weakness,
follow those stripped to almost nothing;
the ragtag bunch who have lost nothing,
running to collect flowery branches
to welcome guests to the ruined stones.

I was stirred, just since, by a cuckoo –
saw it, greyish, elusive;
was lifted – prayed, before I realized –
surprised, in the moment, a wholeness,
the palmed whole, seen by the mystics.

The drought settles over the green meadow,
the water swirls deep in the dry;
the rain man waits, a waiting vessel.

5. Is God Real?

The first elation over: the first long, maddening pain
– that dreary journey – over:

words are fewer; dissertations, fewer:
there are none here to admire!

Is God real? – the only question, ever:
we long for proofs; study the evidence:

the unclamping, recasting, of these weary atoms,
the hidden tomb-act.

The faithless is stoic, stark:
he and I, lordless exiles, tossed on cold seas.

The mind bounces off that vast emptiness:
what good are my prayers in the world?

6. The Desert

– No knowing – say the saints –
that is the desert:

carving of light and space – too huge, mostly;
far-down waters, unheard:

how uncertain, the clarities,
the other side of death, the unvisited –

the sloughing off of this nerve-web,
these deep wounds of mind.

We are all poor things, say the saints,
muddy channels, weeds catching at the quick
                                        prayerfish.

7. Washing the Feet of the Poor

I am disposed to aloneness:
should I be washing the feet of the poor?

– Francis, covered in dust, kissing the leper;
Brother Juniper, split with buffeting,

the holy fool; he longed for nothing but obedience –
he was clear water.

It is old as clay, the long, long abyss-bridge,
building itself as we go –

the kiss, the wasted scaly arms;
the kicks, the tossing, the shouts; the solitudes.

The whole, the little thing –
we are space, mostly: here, plant my foot.

8. Patterns of Stones

People come, leaving food: they want my prayers.
I watch them walk back, over the old sheep-bitten ways.

I want simplicity:
they snarl my path, these shuffles of hands, hopes –

again, again, I am reflected
out of their eyes, fear that –

the pride of austerity,
the dream of shrined bones under the hill.

The intent gaze, undisturbed by footsteps –
a day well spent:

– intent upon what? say the saints –
what relics, what barrows? what patterns of stones?

9. Sanctuary

This sanctuary of hill, tussock, boulder:
the tired saints –

I am pulled up, over and over,
spun round, by the shoulder, to the voices,

the footsteps, traipsing through creation.
What else are we for? say the saints: –

God, outside mass, the unknit:
God the irritant, scuffling through the rocks.

10. The Shadow

The long shadows of evening, how beautiful!
the shadow of us, how ambiguous:

the deep, wracked garden,
where only God walks –

touches dark boles, but beyond knowing.
– What are we, at the roots?

Are we iron of old bleak winter?
Are God's prints there?

The core of stone, ice, holding out;
God, powerless, keeping to his laws: –

we have built the shadow, over the generations.
The earth must tilt –

into the sun, into death:
life's tiny thaw: then the timeless untying, the meltwater.

11. Certain Rare Lights

– It is not evil so much,
as a sense of this unsized clay,

of almost-solid time –
density ploughing through density.

Matter's fitful components, speeding through lead
– here-there –
the scrunched-up tennis ball of the universe! –

the molecules of Christ, whirling somewhere –
Chrestus*, stirring it –

God, pressed into nerve,
starving alveoli; the deepest cellars of mind –

cellars below cellars,
and the rats, how they maul!

Thrown back on God, his doubts:
it is unavoidable aridness;
the path over the chasm seen in certain rare lights –

the desert-trudge to the edge,
the lenses fiddling; playing, lonely, with light.

*as Christ is referred to by Suetonius, the Roman historian

Acknowledgements

Acknowledgements are due to the editors of the following publications where some of these poems first appeared: *Acumen, Along the Line* anthology (Edited by Roger Garfitt, published by The Community College, Bishop's Castle, 1996) *Journal of Anglo-Scandinavian Poetry, Lines Review, New Welsh Review, Orbis, Poetry Review, Poetry Wales, Poet's Voice, Stand, Staple, Summoning the Sea* anthology (The University of Salzburg,1996).